That's not funny, Bunny,!

by
Bethany Rose Hines

IMAGINE THAT

Licensed exclusively to Imagine That Publishing Ltd
Tide Mill Way, Woodbridge, Suffolk, IP12 1AP, UK
www.imaginethat.com
Copyright © 2023 Imagine That Group Ltd
Manufacturer's representative, Eurolink Europe Compliance Limited,
25 Herbert Place, Dublin D02 AY86, Republic of Ireland
All rights reserved
2 4 6 8 9 7 5 3 1
Manufactured in China

Written and illustrated by Bethany Rose Hines

ISBN 978-1-78445-580-4

A catalogue record for this book is available from the British Library

'For my family,' Lots of love Beth

Bunny just wanted
to be different.
He was always dressing
up in silly clothes,
trying to impress
his friends.

Bunny twirled
and swirled
like a
beautiful
ballerina.

But his friends only said,
'That's not funny, Bunny!'

Bunny just loved wearing
silly hats and
funny wigs.

But his friends only said, 'That's not funny, Bunny!'

Bunny put on
a cape and became
a superhero!

But his friends only said,
'That's not funny, Bunny!'

Bunny dressed up as the sun, the moon and the planets.

But his friends only said,
'That's not funny, Bunny!'

He puffed out his chest like a great big, hairy bear.

But his friends only said, 'That's not funny, Bunny!'

Bunny dressed up as his favourite treat -

a strawberry cupcake!

Although his friends thought he looked delicious, still they only said, 'That's not funny, Bunny!'

Bunny was sad. He couldn't seem to do anything to impress his friends.

'Don't be sad,' said Fox. 'I love your soft, velvety ears just the way they are!'

'And I love your fluffy, bouncy tail just the way it is!' said Cat.

'And I love your big heart just the way it is!' said Deer.

Bunny was so happy!
He didn't have to try
to impress anyone at all.
All of his friends loved him
just the way he was.